# MICHAEL GARLAND

# THE GREAT Easter Egg HUNT

A **LOOK AGAIN** Book

**DUTTON CHILDREN'S BOOKS**

*New York*

*Library of Congress Cataloging-in-Publication Data*

Garland, Michael, date.

The great Easter egg hunt / by Michael Garland.—1st ed.

p. cm.

Summary: When Tommy follows the instructions his aunt left him, he is led to several Easter surprises.

ISBN 0-525-47357-2

[1. Easter—Fiction. 2. Picture puzzles. 3. Stories in rhyme.] I. Title.

PZ8.3.G185Gr 2005

[E]—dc22   2004052794

Published in the United States by Dutton Children's Books,

a division of Penguin Young Readers Group

345 Hudson Street, New York, New York 10014

www.penguin.com

Manufactured in China

First Edition

1 3 5 7 9 10 8 6 4 2

*Dear Reader,*

*This book is a puzzle—*
*A hide-and-seek game.*
*There's more folly and fun here*
*Than fortune or fame.*

*Some letters are hiding,*
*And it's your job to seek.*
*They spell something out*
*If you know where to peek.*

*You'll see cute little chicks*
*And lambs all around.*
*They're not hard to spy,*
*And they like to be found.*

*Count all the eggs made*
*Of rubies and gold.*
*Add up chocolate bunnies*
*And bonnets so bold.*

*Check the book's covers—*
*The front and the back.*
*Most things are well hidden,*
*So try to keep track.*

*Take a pencil and paper*
*And carefully look.*
*Make a list of the things*
*That you find in this book.*

*My list's at the end;*
*Take yours and compare.*
*If the two don't agree,*
*There's no need to despair.*

*Look again at these pages,*
*And as you go through,*
*You'll see, if you're careful,*
*My numbers are true.*

*—Aunt Jeanne*

Tommy woke up early on Easter morning and found a note from his favorite aunt.

Dear Tommy,

Hello! Happy Easter!
It's that great time of year.
Follow the bunny,
And he'll lead you here.

He's a funny old hare
With a striking pink vest.
Stay close on his trail,
And he'll do the rest.

—Aunt Jeanne

Tommy dashed across the yard and burst through the hedges in time to see the rabbit darting down a path in the woods. He paused just long enough to read the note tied to the hedge.

*Go down the path*
*That turns into a maze.*
*Getting lost is too easy—*
*There are so many ways.*

*Stay close on the heels*
*Of that cute little bunny.*
*I can promise you'll like*
*What you find more than money.*

BUONA PASQUA

At the end of the path, Tommy found a deep hole in the ground. There was a note lying by the edge.

*Hop right in—*
*You'll soon know why.*
*This hole in the ground*
*Is a hole in the sky!*

*You'll enter a world*
*Where it's Easter all year.*
*A basket of treats*
*Is the thing to hold dear.*

*W*hoosh . . . *thump!* The rabbit hit the ground running, with Tommy right behind.
As he ran along the path, Tommy almost stepped on another note.

Look up at this building.

What words do you see?

There's a message in letters—

Your mind holds the key.

BOLDOG HÚSVÉTI ÜNNEPEKET

As Tommy entered the Easter egg factory, he grabbed the note that was pinned to the door. He read it as he ran along.

Which came first—
The chicken or the egg?
You're falling behind,
So start shaking a leg!

The rabbit bounded up the steps of a building carved entirely out of chocolate. There was another note lying at the entrance.

I **know** you love chocolate—
Please come on inside.
It'll melt in your mouth,
So just open up wide.

Tommy couldn't believe what he saw! He wanted to take a big bite, but he didn't know quite where to start on the ten-foot-tall bunny. As Tommy nibbled on the giant ear, he spotted another note.

Chocolate bunnies like this
Are the best to be found.
Listen close while you eat
For a funny new sound.

*H*iss! *Pop! Boink! Splat!* . . . *Hiss! Pop! Boink! Splat!* What was that racket?
It was the great Jelly Bean Machine! So *this* is how they make them, thought Tommy.

*Catch a whole bunch—*
*You're quick and you're young.*
*Can you name all the flavors*
*That you taste on your tongue?*

The Easter-basket assembly line filled the long building from end to end.
The workers labored furiously as the baskets whipped by.

Add a few eggs
And a colorful bow.
But don't eat the grass—
It's there just for show.

Your next destination
Is no cause for dread.
You'll find something there
That goes on your head.

An Easter stroll

Is not just a walk.

A girl needs a hat

To make people talk.

Tommy saw the rabbit leave the shop. He followed him onto Fifth Avenue and into the middle of the Easter Parade. Tommy read the note attached to a lamppost.

Join the procession
Of this Easter throng.
Can you find all the things
That just don't belong?

A beautiful boulevard led toward a grand, egg-shaped palace. Tommy found an encouraging note stuck to the first statue.

*You're getting closer!*
*In no time you'll see*
*That the furry white rabbit*
*Has brought you to me.*

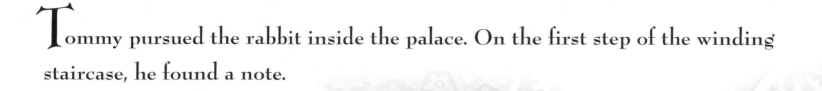

Tommy pursued the rabbit inside the palace. On the first step of the winding staircase, he found a note.

*Don't worry the whys*
*Or the wheres or the whos.*
*Speed it on up!*
*Hit those steps with your shoes!*

*There's a great big surprise*
*At the end of this quest.*
*It's all been arranged by*
*The aunt you love best.*

Dear Reader,

Now that you have reached the end of this book, have you found everything there was to find? Don't forget to look on the title page, the front and back covers, and this page, too! • There are 28 lambs, 67 chicks, 36 chocolate rabbits, and 45 Easter bonnets. (Don't forget to count my hat every time you see it!) • Can you find all the special golden Easter eggs set with red rubies? There are 18 of them. • I am hiding somewhere in each scene—did you spot me every time? • Did you see the hidden "Happy Easter" messages in 14 different languages? Turkish: "Mutlu Paskalya." Korean: "Joun buhwaljol deseyo." French: "Joyeuses Pâques." Italian: "Buona Pasqua." Croatian: "Sretan Uskrs." Hungarian: "Boldog Husveti Ünnepeket." German: "Frohe Ostern." Dutch: "Gelukkig Paasfeest." Portuguese: "Boa Pascoa." Russian: "Schastlivoi Paskhi." Polish: "Wesolych swiat." Greek: "Kalo Pascha." Spanish: "Felices Pascuas." Chinese: "Fu huo jie kuai le." • Were you able to spot all the hidden letters that spell out HAPPY EASTER? • Did you find the message I hid for Tommy on the giant egg next to the Easter egg factory entrance? It says: "The Great Easter Bunny Awaits You." (Hint: Look at the vertical rows of letters from top to bottom.) You should also see (horizontally) Tommy's name along with mine.• How many things did you find in the Easter parade that belong to different holidays? You should have seen a Halloween witch, a ghost with a jack-o'-lantern head, a black cat, a Valentine's Day cupid, Santa Claus and Rudolph the Red-Nosed Reindeer, a Thanksgiving turkey, a St. Patrick's Day leprechaun, as well as George Washington and Abraham Lincoln. • Come back anytime— the Great Easter Bunny loves visitors!

—Aunt Jeanne